FOR JOE, JACKSON AND MAUDE

She sells sea-shells on the sea-shore,
The shells she sells are sea-shells, I'm sure,
For if she sells sea-shells on the sea-shore
Then I'm sure she sells sea-shore shells.

TERRY SULLIVAN 1909

PUFFIN BOOKS

UK | USA | Canada | Ireland | Australia | India | New Zealand | South Africa

Puffin Books is part of the Penguin Random House group of companies
whose addresses can be found at global.penguinrandomhouse.com.

www.penguin.co.uk   www.puffin.co.uk   www.ladybird.co.uk

Penguin
Random House
UK

First published 2023
001

Printed in China

The authorized representative in the EEA is Penguin Random House Ireland,
Morrison Chambers, 32 Nassau Street, Dublin D02 YH68

A CIP catalogue record for this book is available from the British Library

ISBN: 978-0-241-46988-0

All correspondence to: Puffin Books, Penguin Random House Children's
One Embassy Gardens, 8 Viaduct Gardens, London SW11 7BW

MIX
Paper from
responsible sources
FSC® C018179
FSC
www.fsc.org

The FOSSIL HUNTER

KATE WINTER

PUFFIN

MARY ANNING'S LIFE

FOSSILS & CURIOS

Mary is too poor to go to school. Her father teaches her how to find fossils to sell to wealthy tourists.

pages 10–11

A STRANGE BEAST, 1811

Mary's brother Joseph finds the fossil of an ichthyosaur

pages 14–15

HOW THE WORLD BEGAN

Scientists begin to question the history of the world.

pages 20–21

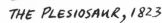

THE PLESIOSAUR, 1823

Mary finds her next big discovery.

pages 32–33

BORN 1799

Mary Anning is born in Lyme Regis on 21 May 1799.

pages 8–9

FOSSIL HUNTERS

After her father dies in 1810, Mary and her brother, Joseph, rely on fossils to provide an income for the family.

pages 12–13

A THIRST FOR KNOWLEDGE

Mary studies to find out more about her ichthyosaur.

pages 16–17

THE BIRCH AUCTION, 1820

A friend helps Mary and her family when they fall on hard times.

pages 30–31

THE GEOLOGICAL SOCIETY

Scientists investigate Mary's plesiosaur but she is not welcomed.

pages 34–35

PHANEROZOIC AEON
541 MILLION YEARS AGO – NOW

Fossils and layers of rocks tell the story of Earth's history, beginning over 4 billion years ago. But it was during the Phanerozoic Aeon that plant and animal life exploded on Earth. This aeon is home to the dinosaurs . . . and to a special young woman named Mary Anning.

PALAEOZOIC 541 – 252 MILLION YEARS AGO

During the Palaezoic Era, plants and reptiles began to move out of the sea and on to the land.

CAMBRIAN	541 – 487	MILLION YEARS AGO
ORDOVICIA	487 – 443	MILLION YEARS AGO
SILURIA	443 – 419	MILLION YEARS AGO
DEVONIAN	419 – 358	MILLION YEARS AGO
CARONIFEROUS	358 – 298	MILLION YEARS AGO
PERMIAN	298 – 252	MILLION YEARS AGO

A LIFE CUT SHORT

Mary dies at age forty-seven, on 9 March 1847.

pages 56–57

MARY'S LEGACY

Mary played an important role in scientific history.

pages 74–75

THE PTEROSAUR

Mary finds a fossil of a flying reptile.

pages 46–47

A TRIP TO LONDON

Mary visits London and sees her fossils in museums.

pages 40–41

OUT OF HISTORY

Many people, like Mary, were written out of scientific history.

pages 36–37

FOSSIL COLLECTORS

Mary's reputation as a talented palaeontologist rose.

pages 70–71

IMPORTANT DISCOVERIES

Mary made many important discoveries during her lifetime.

pages 52–53

THE SHOP AT BROAD STREET, 1826

Mary returns to Lyme Regis and buys her own shop.

pages 44–45

A REMARKABLE FIND

Notorious scientist Georges Cuvier doubts Mary's discovery.

pages 38–39

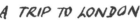

ANNING'S FOSSIL depot

MESOZOIC 252–66 MILLION YEARS AGO

The Mesozoic Era is known as the "Age of the Reptiles". Dinosaurs dominated the land for around 165 million years.

TRIASSIC	252–201 MILLION YEARS AGO
JURASSIC	201–145 MILLION YEARS AGO
CRETACEOUS	145–66 MILLION YEARS AGO

CENOZOIC 66 MILLION YEARS AGO – NOW

The Cenozoic Era is known as the "Age of the Mammals".

PALEOGENE	66–23 MILLION YEARS AGO
NEOGENE	23–2.5 MILLION YEARS AGO
QUATERNARY	2.5 MILLION YEARS AGO – NOW

Some of the fossils Mary found were shiny
like metal, or coiled in a spiral like a snake.
Some were long, pointy and smooth.

Mary used a special hammer to crack
open rocks and find fossils inside.

8

Over two hundred years ago, a young girl called Mary Anning lived in
Lyme Regis, on the south coast of England. Her family were poor, so she and
her brother, Joseph, collected seashells and fossils they found on the beach
and sold them to wealthy tourists.

Mary's favourite place to be was down by the sea. She would search the beach
for popular fossils like snakestones and devil's toenails. These fossils were
found washed up on the shoreline and hidden in the cliffs.

Mary knew there was more to these fossils than merely old shells
or dead sea creatures. She hadn't seen anything like them living
in the sea or in the books she had read.

Lyme Regis is part of the Jurassic Coast,
which is now a World Heritage Site
known for its amazing rocks, fossils
and landforms.

Mary's father taught her all about the fossils
on the beach and how to find them.

9

The tourists who came to Lyme Regis were fascinated by these unusual finds. A journey to the seaside was like an exotic holiday, and the shells and spiralling stones were souvenirs of this very different place. The fossils Mary sold were known as curios; they had different names which often hinted at some myth or legend.

Fossils and Curios

ICHTHYOSAUR VERTEBRAE

Verteberries were thought to be crocodile teeth but were actually the backbones of an ichthyosaur – a marine reptile of the Jurassic Period.

AMMONITES

The legend of St Hilda's snakestones tells the story of serpents or people turned to stone. In fact, they are an extinct type of mollusc – a bit like a squid but with an external hard, coiled shell. Some were huge!

GRYPHAEA ARCUATA

Devil's toenails are an extinct oyster-like mollusc with a thick shell. People thought these strange objects could cure tired and achy bones.

COPROLITE

Bezoar stones were once believed to have magical properties, capable of curing any poison. Some are in fact a type of fossilized poo!

ECHINOIDS

Sea urchins were spiny marine invertebrates that lived on the seabed. They were considered to be lucky, with magical powers.

TYPES of FOSSILS

Body fossils are the remains of an animal or plant – like bones or leaves – which show us what it looked like.

Trace fossils show us the activities of an animal, such as footprints and trackways.

BELEMNITES

Devil's fingers were said to have been thrown from the sky during thunderstorms and, in powdered form, could cure sore eyes. They are also an extinct mollusc, similar to ammonites but with an internal cone-like skeleton.

MARCASITE

Angel or Cupid wings are actually minerals found in rocks rather than fossils. These pretty crystals were popular with tourists, much like the shiny and enchanting fool's gold.

DAPEDIUM POLITUM

John Dory's bones was a popular name for this ancient fossilized fish. It lived 180–150 million years ago, in the Jurassic Period.

PALEAOCOMA EGERTONI

Brittle stars are a type of starfish with long wavy legs that looked very pretty in a Georgian display cabinet.

CRINOIDS

Sea lilies aren't flowers but animals related to starfish and sea urchins that first evolved 480 million years ago.

CARBONIFEROUS CRINOIDS / PENTACRINITES

St Cuthbert's beads come from a marine animal called a crinoid. The bead-like plates that made up the stem were strung together as necklaces and were also known as "fairy money".

When Mary was just eleven years old, her father died after falling from Black Ven, a big cliff in Lyme Regis. Mary, her brother, Joseph, and their mother, Molly, were left without any income. Mary had to rely on selling fossils to get enough money for her family to eat but also to pay off the many debts her father had left behind.

The best time for finding fossils was in the winter months when the sea was rough. Mary and Joseph would often leave the house in the cold early hours of the morning, hoping to be the first to the cliffs to find the treasures left by the sea.

A Strange beast, 1811

Today we found the most exciting thing!
There was a storm in the night so me and Joseph
rushed down to the beach. The sea had dragged up
loads of snakestones, some big ones that would sell
well once cleaned up and polished.

We went to the cliff and Joseph noticed something poking
out of the rock. At first, we thought it was another kind
of snakestone but, as we scraped away at the mud, we
saw it was an enormous skull!

It's bigger than anything we've ever seen before.

What kind of strange
beast is this?

Joseph and Mary found something quite extraordinary.

They carefully dug out a huge skull with their special tools.

Later they needed help to get the whole body out of the cliff.

Back home, Mary cleaned each of the fossilized bones.

She gradually uncovered the most astonishing beast.

It had flippers and a tail like a dolphin, but the head of a crocodile – with huge eyes and very sharp teeth!

Mary's discovery was unlike anything she had ever seen before. It didn't look anything like the sea life she knew from Lyme Regis. And when she searched in books, she could not find any creature that compared to her monster.

News reached London of the new discovery by the young Anning children,
and a name was given to it: *Ichthyosaur*. Scientists and scholars
wanted to see the creature and find out what Mary knew.

Where had she discovered it? What kind of rock was it found in?
Were there other large creatures to be found there?

Mary had the same thirst for knowledge as these educated men.
She had learned to read and write at an early age and wanted to
know as much as she could about these creatures from the past.

Mary, like many people at that time, believed that God created the world in six days, roughly 6,000 years ago. But the finding of fossils made some people question their beliefs. Why would God create these fearsome creatures? And why would he make creatures that no longer exist? Scientists began to put forward different theories about the origins of our world.

We now know that the Earth is over *4 billion years old*, but back then people had lots of different ideas . . .

Some people believed that fossils were the remains
of creatures that had died during the Flood because,
in the Bible, Moses says that all creatures were
wiped out, except the few saved in Noah's Ark.

But the discoveries that Mary and other
fossil hunters made were clues that helped
us to understand the layers of history that
led to the world as we know it today.

Mary couldn't have known that the ichthyosaur she had discovered was part of this great evolutionary journey that began millions of years ago. Once, her creature would have swam in a sea that covered the whole of the Dorset coast, and beyond. Her discovery played an important part in helping scientists develop their understanding of evolution, the history of our world and how it came to be.

Around 2,500 million years ago, simple organisms, consisting of a single cell, gradually evolved into organisms composed of multiple cells.

About 541 million years ago, shelled creatures evolved. Variations of these are still around today.

Around 500 million years ago, algae grew in the sea that eventually gave rise to the plants we know today.

Around 4,000 million years ago,
bacteria, the first living things, appeared
in the sea. After another few million years
cyanobacteria started to create oxygen
in a process called photosynthesis.
This created a rise in levels of oxygen
in the Earth's atmosphere, leading
to more complex forms of life.

We now understand that in the Mesozoic Era, 250 million years ago,
the world was connected in one big landmass called PANGAEA. Over time,
this supercontinent evolved to become the world as we know it now.

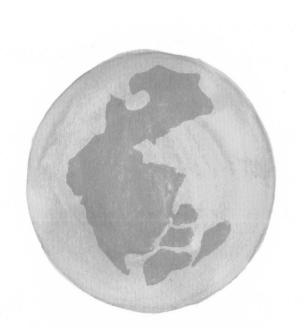

PANGAEA

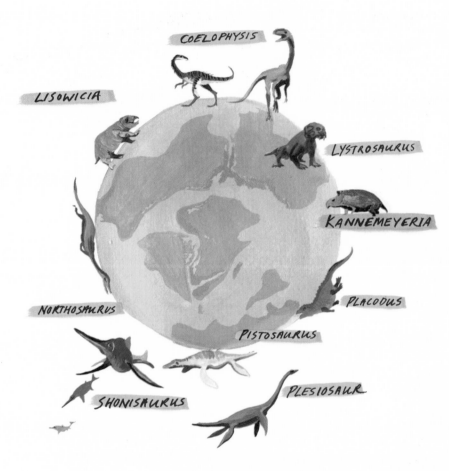

THE TRIASSIC PERIOD
252 – 201 MILLION YEARS AGO

The Triassic Period was a time of great change.
The climate was hot and dry, with large areas covered
in deserts. Life outside of the oceans began to flourish
and the first dinosaurs appeared on Earth.

THE JURASSIC PERIOD
201 – 145 MILLION YEARS AGO

In the Jurassic Period, Pangaea split into two huge continents. With more land exposed to water, the climate changed rapidly and created huge forests. With more to eat, dinosaurs became colossal and the first flying reptiles evolved.

THE CRETACEOUS PERIOD
145 – 66 MILLION YEARS AGO

Very slowly, the land separated into the continents we recognize today. More species evolved, including birds, mammals and insects. Bees helped pollination and spread flowering plants. As the environment changed, there were more dinosaurs than ever before . . .

About 200 million years ago, ichthyosaurs and other marine reptiles dominated the oceans, while dinosaurs roamed on land and flying reptiles soared in the sky.

About 480 million years ago,
tailed creatures shaped like tadpoles
developed into fish. Fish then grew
limbs and the first amphibians crept
up on to the land.

After her major ichthyosaur discovery, Mary continued to find fossils to sell
to the scientists who had flocked to Lyme Regis. But in 1819 the Annings were
in a bad way. Mary hadn't found any important fossils in over a year and the
family were forced to sell off their furniture to pay the rent.

Thomas James Birch had long been a friend and customer of Mary's, so when he heard about the family's problems he decided to sell his entire collection of fossils to help them – many of which Mary had found.

GOING, GOING, GONE!

The auction was held by Mr Bullock on 15 May 1820. Mary's ichthyosaur was bought by the Royal College of Surgeons for £100. The entire sale made almost £400 – almost £40,000 today! This money supported Mary's family at a time of great need, and raised her profile as a fossil hunter and palaeontologist.

Mary's next discovery was even bigger . . .

On 10 December 1823, at the bottom of Black Ven cliff, Mary worked through the night to uncover a strange creature.

It was almost three metres long, with the head of a lizard, the neck of a serpent, the teeth of a crocodile and the paddles of a whale.

Mary had found an almost complete skeleton of a plesiosaur – another huge marine reptile of the prehistoric ocean.

Mary carefully prepared her plesiosaur and packed it into a huge wooden box.
It was shipped to London for scientific investigation at the Geological Society.
It was here that fossils and rocks from all over Europe were discussed and debated.

When it finally arrived, it took a gigantic effort to lift the heavy box into the
building. Giving up at the entrance hall, the scientists unpacked the monstrous
creature, peering at it in glimmering candlelight.

Upstairs, William Conybeare presented the fossil of
Plesiosaurus giganteus, even using some of Mary's drawings.
But he did not once mention her name.

Reverend Conybeare, who I have so often shared ideas with, has written about my plesiosaur. But he has not once mentioned me as the person responsible for this creature's discovery! How can he treat me this way? Just because I am a woman and, in his eyes, a lesser being than him.

Mary was not the only woman to be written out of scientific history. There were other women at that time who did great work behind the scenes. What makes Mary's story stand out is that she came from a tough working-class background.

Mary made amazing discoveries and contributed to the learning of others, all while trying to find the rent and enough food for her family. Many working-class men, too, would find fossils for rich men to claim and name as their own.

In the 1800s the collecting of fossils was fashionable and those who had the time and money to spare could focus their energies on pursuing science. Britain had made lots of money from plantations in the Caribbean, benefitting from the evil practice of slavery. The ability of wealthy men and women to make scientific discoveries was only made possible through the sacrifice and mistreatment of others.

When word reached the rest of Europe about the discovery of a complete plesiosaur,
the French palaeontologist Georges Cuvier was suspicious. From the drawings and
description he had seen, Cuvier suspected that Mary had invented the creature,
adding in extra bones from other beasts to make it seem even more fantastical.
It was not uncommon for fossils to be discovered as fakes.

How could Cuvier doubt my find? I would never lie to further my career or fool the scientists. I want to find the truth and to be acknowledged for my part. I wish that one day women like me, of my social standing, will be recognized for our intellect and contribution.

But once Cuvier came to see the specimen for himself, he saw it was indeed a remarkable find.

In 1829 Mary was invited to visit London by geologists Roderick and Charlotte Murchison. She likely travelled by ship — perhaps on the same boat that had carried her beloved plesiosaur only a few years before.

Sailing up the River Thames, Mary would have passed bustling warehouses full of sugar, tea and spices. After passing Billingsgate Market and the Tower of London her boat would have docked near London Bridge.

What would Mary have thought of this crowded, smoky city?

London was the largest city in the world in the early nineteenth century – a huge port, teeming with people. As well as great wealth, it was also a city full of poverty and crime. Coming from the small seaside town of Lyme Regis, Mary would have been amazed by all she saw.

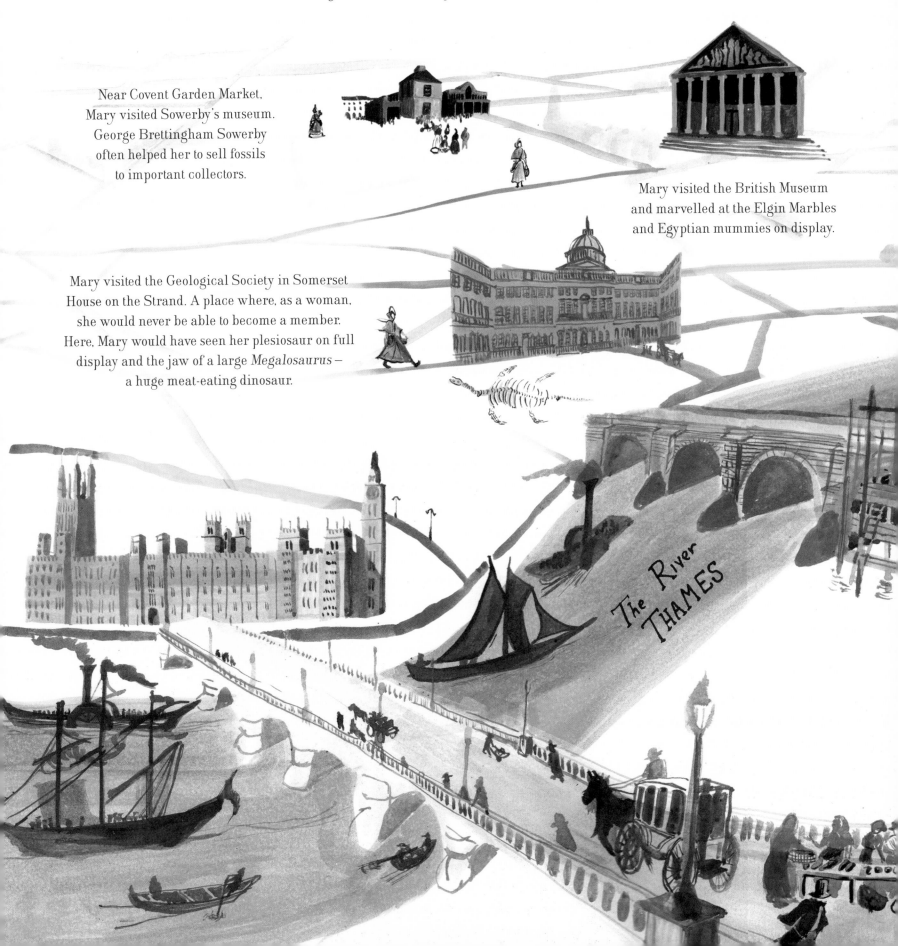

Near Covent Garden Market, Mary visited Sowerby's museum. George Brettingham Sowerby often helped her to sell fossils to important collectors.

Mary visited the British Museum and marvelled at the Elgin Marbles and Egyptian mummies on display.

Mary visited the Geological Society in Somerset House on the Strand. A place where, as a woman, she would never be able to become a member. Here, Mary would have seen her plesiosaur on full display and the jaw of a large *Megalosaurus* – a huge meat-eating dinosaur.

The River THAMES

At the time of Mary's visit, Trafalgar Square had not yet been built – there were no cast bronze lions to climb or Nelson's statue peering down. However, Mary might have known that an elephant-like mammoth had been found in nearby Charing Cross in 1690. Over 250 years later, in the 1950s, fossils of prehistoric animals – hippos, lions, an elephant with straight tusks, and other creatures – were found beneath Trafalgar Square, where Mary and thousands of others had passed.

Wherever I have walked, on the beach in Lyme or even in the big
and busy city of London, I've always wondered what could be
buried beneath my feet. Living forms stomping, growling and
existing millions of years ago . . .

When Mary returned home, life got better for the Annings.
They managed to move up the road, away from the seafront
to Broad Street. Here they were able to get a proper shop
from which to sell their fossils.

ANNING'S
FOSSIL
depot

By now Mary had become very well known among palaeontologists. Her shop had also turned into a tourist attraction and she was able to make a good living selling snakestones, or rather ammonites, as they had then become known, and belemnites, the "devil's fingers" she had found as a child.

Pterosaurs lived between 226–266 million years ago, in the Mesozoic Era, spread widely around the world.

The largest flying animal that ever lived was a pterosaur called *Quetzalcoatlus*, which had a wingspan of up to 12 metres. This huge beast didn't have any teeth and swallowed its prey whole.

Their wings were similar to those of a bat, but they glided and flapped up and down like birds.

Mary was right: the winged creature was a reptile and flew
in the prehistoric sky, catching fish and building nests just
like the seabirds she saw outside her shop window.

Mary had found the fossil of a pterodactyl —
a flying reptile that lived at the same time
as the dinosaurs. It belonged to a group
called pterosaurs.

In 1828 the early winter storms revealed another
unusual fossilized skeleton – this time with wings.

*I have found a winged creature. It may be a bird except it has
many similar bones to a reptile. So it could have been a flying reptile.*

*Imagine that. What a strange world this must have been all
that time ago with dragon-like creatures flying above your head.
How I wish I could see it for myself!*

The *Tapejara* flew but also walked on all fours, with its wings folded. It had a large crest over its beak that extended back behind the head.

The *Eudimorphodon* looked a bit like a bat. It had three short fingers with sharp claws that came out from both wings.

Flying alongside pterosaurs, the *Archaeopteryx* was a small crow-sized dinosaur, with long feathery wings, related to the infamous *Velociraptor*.

The *Tupandactylus* had an enormous crest – the largest of any known pterosaur. This crest would have been brightly coloured, possibly to scare away rivals or to attract a mate.

In the Cretaceous Period bird-like dinosaurs began to evolve into creatures that were more like birds we recognise today. When dinosaurs became extinct, these early birds were the only group to survive. Some of them evolved to become the birds we know and love today.

Mary found many fossils throughout her life, often with her dog, Tray, by her side. The skull of her first ichthyosaur, now called *Temnodontosaurus platyodon*, and her plesiosaur, now called *Plesiosaurus dolichodeirus*, can be seen at the Natural History Museum in London.

As well as the large creatures, Mary discovered many extraordinary smaller fossils.

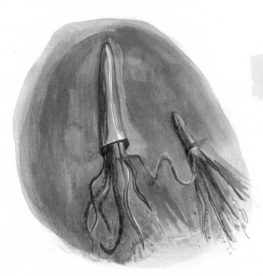

BELEMNOSEPIA

This is a type of cuttlefish that Mary discovered with its ink sac – similar to that of an octopus or squid – still intact.

SQUALORAJA

This fossil was only 45 centimetres long. Mary described it as a skeleton with a head like a pair of scissors and a tail with six claws.

COPROLITE

One of Mary's most important discoveries was that of coprolites: strange lumps of stone.
They felt heavy like metal and were very different from normal pebbles. Together with
palaeontologist, William Buckland, Mary realized that these lumpy stones were, in fact, poo!
This was an incredible discovery. They could break into the stones to find out what these Jurassic
creatures ate, discovering scales of fish, like the *Dapedium politum*, and even undigested teeth.

PREHISTORIC DORSET

In 1830 Henry de la Beche painted a watercolour based on Mary's discoveries called
'Duria Antiquior', which means 'a more ancient Dorset'. The painting showed what prehistoric
Dorset might have looked like when the ichthyosaurs and plesiosaurs swam in the sea.
There are some reports that suggest he sold copies of the painting to support Mary in her old age.

Duria Antiquior
by Henry de la Beche

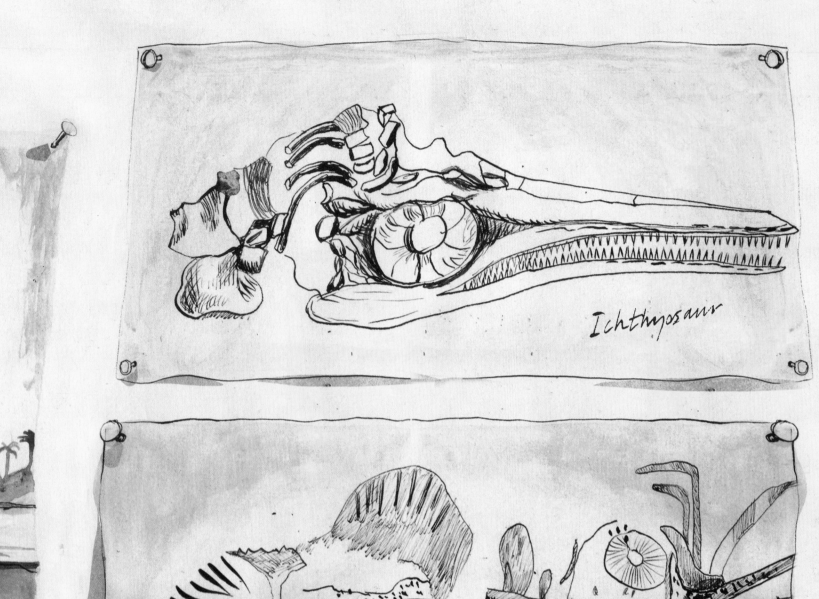

Ichthyosaur

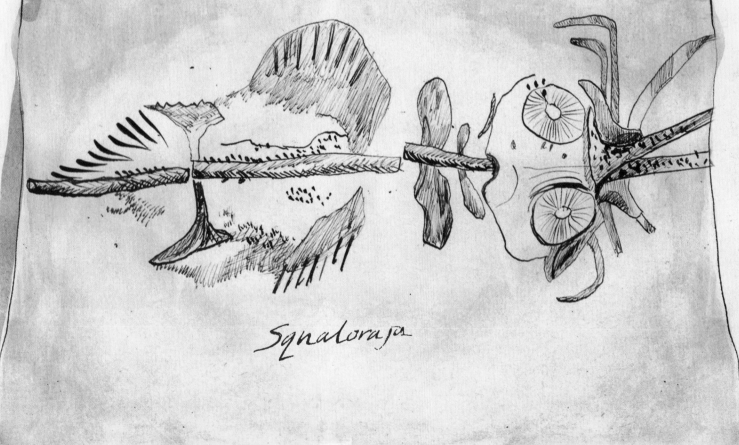

Squaloraja

Mary lived in and out of poverty her whole life. She relied on the sea and cliffs
to provide new discoveries and, as she got older, this dangerous work
of climbing and digging became much harder for her.

As fossils became less rare, people began to lose interest in buying them, and Mary's
income dried up. Her friends tried to help by donating money to her, and a charity called
the British Association for the Advancement of Science raised a yearly income for her.
Even the prime minister was persuaded to donate to the fund. It wasn't much money
for Mary to live on but it was at least some thanks and recognition in her lifetime.
Sadly, Mary fell ill and died at the young age of forty-seven.

Have you ever found something mysterious?
Something where you had no idea what it
was but you had this feeling it was
important, that it held a secret?

Ladies' fingers

Snake stone

Snake stone

Snake stone

Devils toenails

Coral

Snake skin

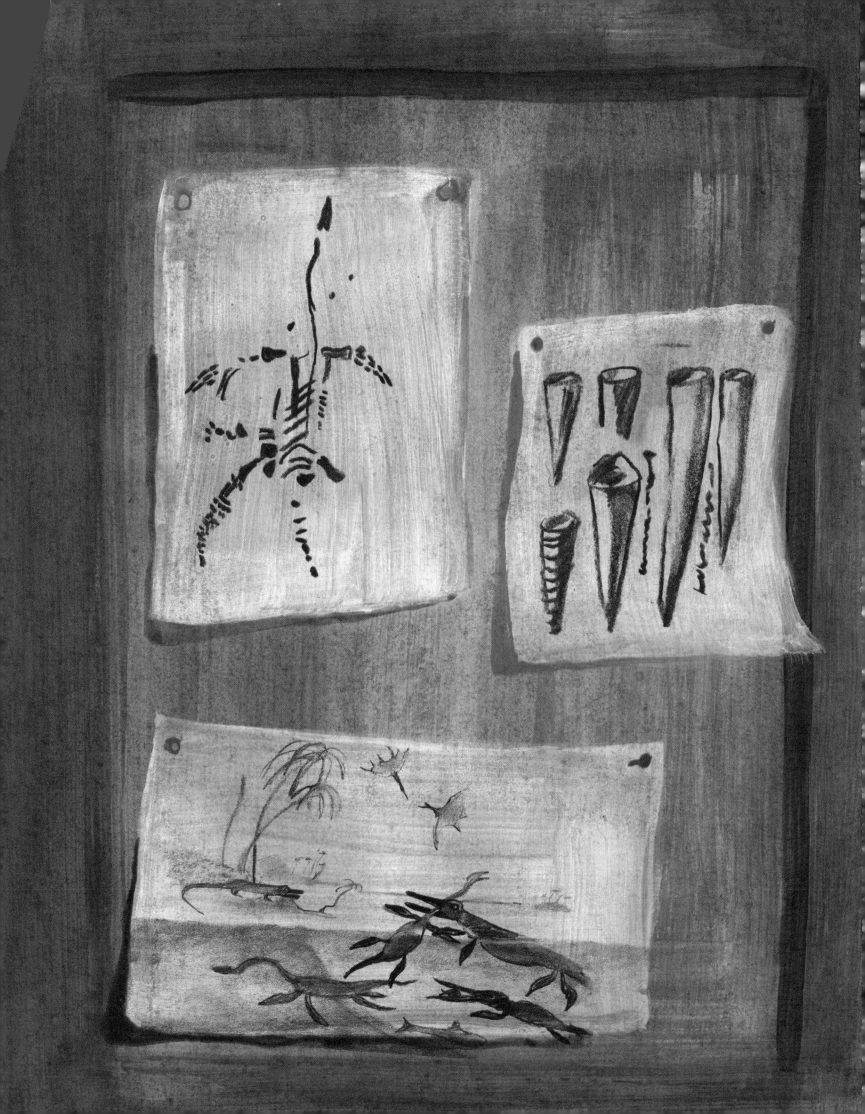

A LOOK INSIDE MARY'S CABINET

AN AUCTION

ORGANISED FOSSILS
FROM THE BLUE LIAS FORMATION
At Lyme and Charmouth,
in Dorsetshire

THE GENUINE
PROPERTY OF COLONEL BIRCH

BY MR. BULLOCK
AT HIS
EGYPTIAN H.
in PICCADILL

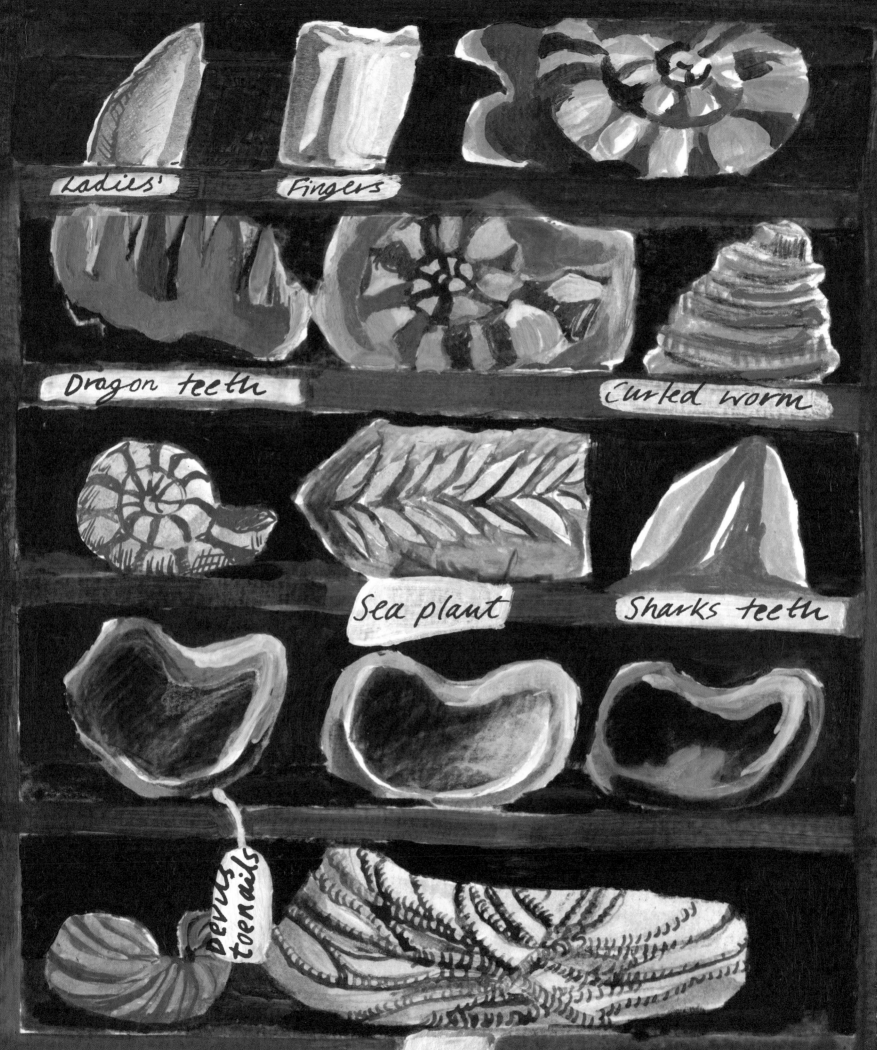

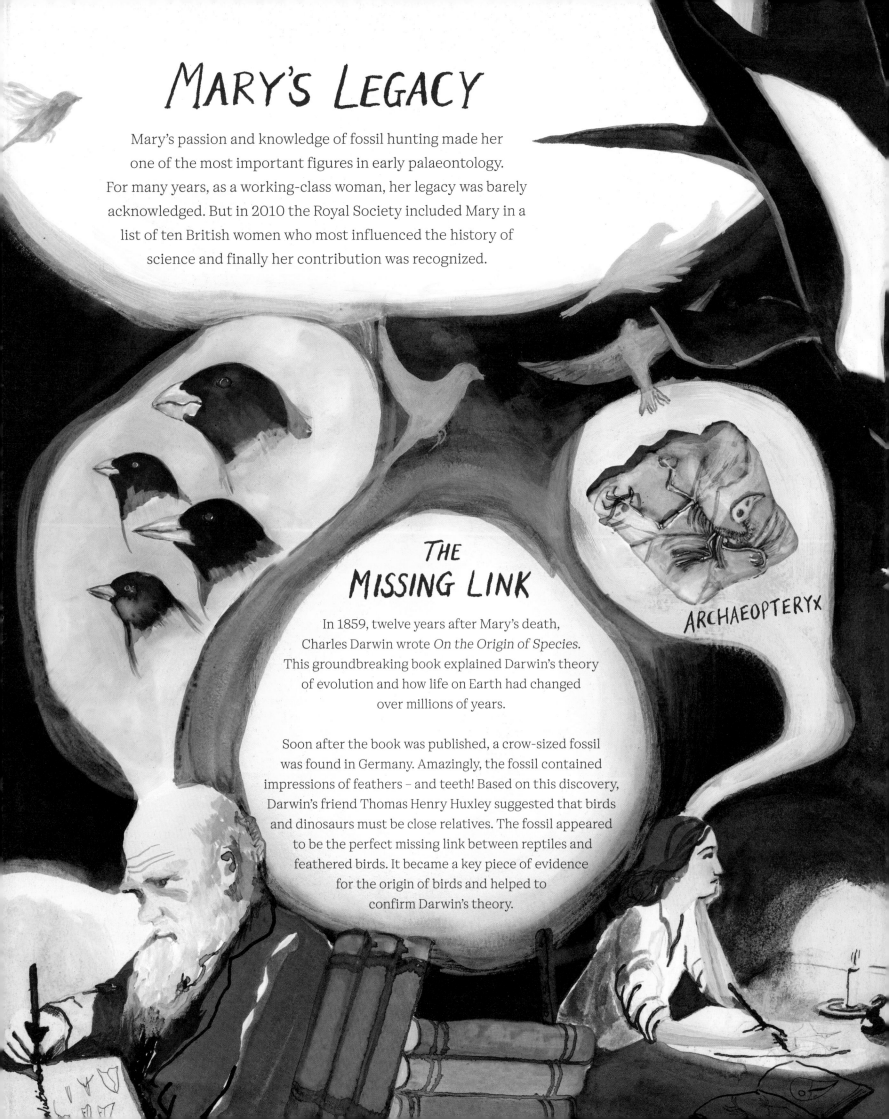

MARY'S LEGACY

Mary's passion and knowledge of fossil hunting made her one of the most important figures in early palaeontology. For many years, as a working-class woman, her legacy was barely acknowledged. But in 2010 the Royal Society included Mary in a list of ten British women who most influenced the history of science and finally her contribution was recognized.

THE MISSING LINK

In 1859, twelve years after Mary's death, Charles Darwin wrote *On the Origin of Species*. This groundbreaking book explained Darwin's theory of evolution and how life on Earth had changed over millions of years.

Soon after the book was published, a crow-sized fossil was found in Germany. Amazingly, the fossil contained impressions of feathers – and teeth! Based on this discovery, Darwin's friend Thomas Henry Huxley suggested that birds and dinosaurs must be close relatives. The fossil appeared to be the perfect missing link between reptiles and feathered birds. It became a key piece of evidence for the origin of birds and helped to confirm Darwin's theory.

ARCHAEOPTERYX

ANNINGASAURA

In the early 1840s Louis Agassiz, a friend of Mary's, named two fossil fish species after her – *Acrodus anningiae* and *Belenostomus anningiae*. He was the only person to recognize her in this way during her lifetime. After her death other animals were named in her honour: a shrimp-like creature *Cytherelloidea anningi*, a mammal-like reptile *Anningia megalops*, and a genus of mollusc *Anningella*. In 2012 palaeontologists Dean Lomax and Judy Massare discovered a new type of ichthyosaur and named it *Ichthyosaurus anningae*.

The plesiosaur *Anningasaura* was first described by Peggy Vincent and Roger Benson.

MARY ANNING ROCKS

In 2018 eleven-year-old Evie and her mum, Anya Pearson, launched "Mary Anning Rocks"! This campaign called for a statue of Mary to recognize her legacy in her home town of Lyme Regis. Sculptor Denise Dutton created a beautiful memorial of Mary Anning and her dog Tray.

WHAT HAPPENED TO THE DINOSAURS?

Since Mary's first early discoveries, new technologies tell us that dinosaurs and prehistoric reptiles lived on Earth until 66 million years ago. Their reign lasted for around 180 million years.

But what happened to them?

ASTEROID ATTACKS

In 1980 scientists suggested that a giant meteor crashed into Earth, wiping out all dinosaurs. Large quantities of iridium, a metal common in meteors, were found above rock layers containing dinosaur fossils. These rocks are from the end of the Cretaceous and start of the Palaeogene or the K-Pg Event. Scientists also pointed to a huge crater along the coast of Mexico where a giant meteorite might have landed. This would have been powerful enough to cause major changes in the Earth's atmosphere.

Another contribution to their mass extinction might have been the eruption of ancient volcanoes, which would have covered vast areas with molten-hot lava and volcanic ash. Such huge eruptions would have filled the air and sky with poisonous gases, resulting in mass extinction of life.

VIOLENT VOLCANOES

What we do know is that around three-quarters of all species were wiped out, including all dinosaurs except those which evolved into birds. Fossil records show us that there have been at least five mass exinctions in Earth's history. By researching these catastrophic episodes, scientists can learn vital lessons about the effects of climate change – and see how life can bounce back.

FOSSIL COLLECTORS

In the early 1800s, there was a growing curiosity about fossils. Just like Mary, scientists questioned what these creatures were and if they had any relation to animals living on the planet now. Each fossil seemed to add a piece to the complex puzzle of understanding life on Earth.

Mary took many scientists on fossil hunts and sold her best finds to these collectors. Some of them became friends but, as a working-class woman, she was never acknowledged in the scientific papers they wrote.

ELIZABETH PHILPOT (1790 – 1857)

Elizabeth was a wealthy woman who lived in Lyme Regis with her sisters. Elizabeth often spoke with Mary about her finds and lent her books about geology and zoology.

WILLIAM AND MARY BUCKLAND (1784 – 1856)   (1797 – 1857)

The Bucklands were passionate about fossils and were very interested in Mary's discoveries. They wrote and illustrated a book called *Geology and Mineralogy* (1836), which tried to uncover the origins of these prehistoric creatures.

HENRY THOMAS DE LA BECHE (1796 – 1855)

Henry grew up in Lyme Regis and had known Mary since they were children. He became an important geologist and palaeontologist, and was the first director of the Geological Survey of Great Britain.

CHARLOTTE AND ROBERT MURCHINSON (1788–1869)   (1792 – 1871)

Charlotte was a well-respected geologist who travelled the world with her husband, Roderick, sketching landforms and building up an impressive collection of fossils.

LIEUTENANT COLONEL THOMAS JAMES BIRCH (1768 – 1829)

Thomas James Birch, an officer in the British Army, was a great collector of fossils and bought many of Mary's finds.

REVD WILLIAM CONYBEARE (1787–1857)

Reverend Conybeare was an English geologist, palaeontologist and clergyman. His life's work was to link closely with Mary's as he used her discoveries to advance his own scientific career.

GEORGES CUVIERS (1769 – 1832)

Georges Cuvier, known as the "founding father of palaeontology", was a French zoologist. Mary read his books to compare the fossils she had found with living animals. Although he was very educated, he was an unpleasant man with racist theories.

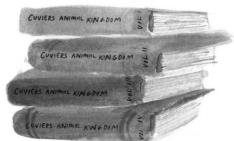

ARCTIC

Some people believed that fossilized bones and shells had to be from a different planet altogether.

Indigenous communities in North America who found fossils passed down creation stories about giant lizards, thunder birds and monster bears by telling them to their children.

In 1676 Reverend Plot discovered an enormous thigh bone, belonging to a *Megalosaurus*. At the time, Plot thought it must have belonged to an ancient species of human giant.

In the 1830s giant dinosaur tracks found in Connecticut, USA were thought to belong to giant wading birds.

In 1824 William Buckland wrote the first official scientific description in Europe of a dinosaur bone. This described the fossilized jawbone of a *Megalosaurus*.

A PREHISTORIC WORLD

Throughout human history, people have studied fossils to make sense of the world. Creation stories were passed down through generations, great myths and legends were told, and some ancient scientists had some really clever ideas . . .

ATLANTIC OCEAN

Some of the earliest dinosaurs from the Triassic Period were found in the Valley of the Moon, Argentina.

OCEAN

In 1842 scientist Richard Owen developed the theory that the mysterious bones being found all shared similar features and were unlike any animal alive on the planet at the time. He coined the name "dinosaur" for this entirely new group of animals, which means "terrible lizards".

Mysterious bones and fossils found in China 2,000 years ago were described in writing as "dragon bones".

The ancient Greeks and Romans developed mythologies about giant creatures as they sought to understand the fossils they found.

The famous thinker Ibn Sina, from medieval Persia, wrote in the 1020s that fossils were the likely result of earthquakes and other natural events.

PACIFIC OCEAN

Shen Kuo, a Chinese scientist from the Song dynasty (960–1279), studied fossils of bamboo and realized that climates changed over time.

In Egypt, the remains of a *Spinosaurus aegyptiacus*, an "enormous river-monster", were first discovered in 1920.

INDIAN OCEAN

In 2018 a shepherd found a dinosaur graveyard in South Africa, with fossils up to 200 million years old.

In Australia, dinosaur tracks have been part of creation mythology for thousands of years. The three-toed tracks in the story of Marala, the Emu Man, are now thought to be those of meat-eating dinosaurs.

73

RECENT DISCOVERIES

Mary had many questions that went unanswered in her lifetime:
What were these creatures? When did they exist?
What happened to them? She was at the dawn of new scientific
discovery and, spurred on by her finds, new technologies
were quickly developed to help answer her questions.

RADIOMETRIC DATING

In the late 1800s scientists began to understand how old
fossils were by looking at atoms in rock layers. Atoms are tiny
particles that exist in all things and, over time, they give off
different levels of radioactivity. The changes in these levels
can be measured in units of time. So, scientists can measure
radioactivity in ancient rock and calculate how much time
has passed. If they know how old the layer of rock is, they can
determine the age of fossils.

MODERN TECHNOLOGIES

Now, scientists have even more tools at their
fingertips. Electron microscopes can reveal the
tiniest details, while X-ray machines can look inside
a fossil. Advanced computer programs can construct
3D representations and show us how extinct animals
may have moved and looked.

GIANT MILLIPEDES
BIG AS CARS ROAMED
NORTHERN ENGLAND

180 MILLION YEARS
OLD SEA MONSTER
FOSSIL FOUND

SCIENTISTS FIND NEW
SPECIES OF FOUR-LEGGED
WHALE THAT LIVED
43 MILLION YEARS AGO

MAJOR FOSSIL FINDS

Over the past fifty years, there have been many significant fossil finds, which have helped us understand even more about these prehistoric creatures.

FOSSIL OF DINOSAUR MID-FIGHT FOUND

In 1971 an amazing fossil discovery in Mongolia revealed a meat-eating *Velociraptor* and a plant-eating *Protoceratops* in combat. This captured moment in time showed how dinosaurs lived and fought.

FOSSIL SHOWS DINOSAURS HAD FUR

In 1996 a *Sinosauropteryx* fossil was discovered in China. This creature appeared to have a layer of fur to keep warm – a bit like the feathers on a bird. This small fuzzy dinosaur also had a red-and-white tail, which gave more information about how dinosaurs might have looked and the colours they were.

FOSSIL REVEALS DINOSAURS WERE GOOD MOTHERS

In the 1990s a fossil known as "good mother lizard" was found in Montana, USA. This fossil of a *Maiasaura* and her babies revealed important evidence about family life and showed that they didn't abandon their young.

FOSSILISED FEATHER FOUND IN RESIN

In 2016 the tail of a *Coelurosaur* was found inside a piece of amber in Myanmar. Amber is a hard yellowish material made from fossilized resin – a sticky substance that oozed from prehistoric trees. The resin captured the tail of this small bird-like dinosaur 99 million years ago. This discovery showed scientists how feathers might have evolved for warmth or mating. We now know that some (but not all) dinosaurs were feathered, that some were able to fly, and that others were ancestors of modern birds.

GLOSSARY

AEONS represent periods of time, lasting millions of years. The history of Earth began with the Hadean Aeon, around 4.5 billion years ago, which was followed by the Archaean Aeon, the Proterozoic Aeon, and the Phanerozoic Aeon, which dates from the Cambrian Period to the present day.

ALGAE are simple organisms often consisting of a single cell. Algae are very important because they generate oxygen, which is needed for all forms of life. Scientists have found algae fossils over a billion years old.

AMPHIBIANS were the first vertebrates (animals with a backbone) to live on land. Examples today include frogs, salamanders and newts. They need water, or a moist environment, to survive.

CYANOBACTERIA are a type of blue-green algae. These simple single-celled organisms create oxygen and make their own food through photosynthesis.

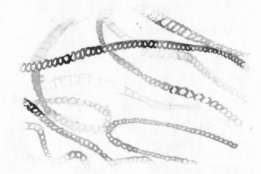

EVOLUTION is a a process of change in living things over a long period of time. Living things that exist today are linked to, and have developed (evolved) from earlier species.

EXTINCTION is the dying-out or disappearance of a species from Earth.

GEOLOGY is a science that studies the evolution and history of Earth. Geologists study rocks, minerals, fossils, landforms and the layers of the Earth's surface.

GEORGIAN refers to the the Georgian era – a period in British history from 1714 to 1837, around the time Mary was alive.

THE JURASSIC COAST stretches from Exmouth in East Devon to Studland Bay in Dorset, UK. The rocks and fossils found there tell us a lot about the Jurassic Period.

MARINE INVERTEBRATES are ocean animals without a backbone, and include starfish, jellyfish, corals and anemones.

MARINE REPTILES are aquatic or semiaquatic, meaning they have adapted for life in the ocean. During the Mesozoic Era, marine reptiles, such as ichthyosaurs, plesiosaurs and mosasaurs, became so well-adapted to life in the ocean that they were incapable of leaving the water. Today, marine reptiles include saltwater crocodiles, sea turtles, marine iguanas and sea snakes.

MINERALS are found naturally on Earth, often in rocks. They can be made from a single element (like gold or silver) or from a combination of elements. The Earth is made up of thousands of different minerals.

MOLLUSCS are a type of invertebrate with a soft body covered by an outer layer, called a mantle. Many live inside a shell. Today's molluscs include slugs, snails, octopuses and oysters.

PALAEONTOLOGY is the study of prehistoric life, from dinosaurs to ancient plants, animals and even micro-organisms. Palaeontologists study fossils to see what our planet was like long ago.

PANGAEA was a supercontinent that existed during the Late Palaeozoic and Early Mesozoic Eras. It eventually split to become the continents we know today.

PHOTOSYNTHESIS is a natural process of plants. It uses sunlight, water and carbon dioxide to create oxygen and food.

POLLINATION is a very important process that allows plants to make new plants. Insects, like bees, take pollen between flowers, which means the plants can make seeds, from which new flowers will grow. Wind and rain, as well as other animals such as birds and bats, can also spread pollen.

SEDIMENT is made up from bits of earth, dirt and rock that have been carried along by water, ice or wind. It settles on top of things. Many organisms that die in the sea are soon buried by sediment.

ZOOLOGY is the scientific study of animals – both living and extinct. Zoologists investigate how animals live, what they eat, and how they interact with each other and their environment.

I COULD NOT HAVE MADE THIS BOOK WITHOUT THE AMAZING TEAM AT PENGUIN. HUGE THANKS GOES TO LARA, ANNA, SOPHIE AND THE BRILLIANT MONICA. I AM FOREVER GRATEFUL TO MY DEAR FRIENDS WONDERFUL HUSBAND JOE AND PATIENT FAMILY. YOUR SUPPORT AND ENCOURAGEMENT HAS KEPT ME GOING. I AM VERY THANKFUL TO DR KATIE COLLINS AND EMMA BERNARD AT THE NATURAL HISTORY MUSEUM FOR THEIR KNOWLEDGE, EXPERTISE AND GUIDANCE. THANKS ALSO TO MY TUTORS AT CAMBRIDGE SCHOOL OF ART WHO HAVE DONE SO MUCH FOR ME AND FOR CHILDRENS BOOK ILLUSTRATION AS A WHOLE. I AM PARTICULARLY INDEBTED TO PAM SMY. I'D FINALLY LIKE TO RAISE A GLASS TO ALL THE ACTIVISTS AND SUPPORTERS OF WOMEN'S RIGHTS, PAST AND PRESENT. THANK YOU FOR FIGHTING FOR A FAIRER WORLD.

THANK YOU